First published in the United States 1986 by
Dial Books for Young Readers
2 Park Avenue · New York, New York 10016
Published in West Germany by Middelhauve-Bilderbuch
Copyright © 1985 by Gertraud Middelhauve Verlag
Printed in West Germany
COBE
First Edition
2 4 6 8 10 9 7 5 3 1

Library of Congress Cataloging-in-Publication Data
Bröger, Achim. The Santa Clauses.
Translation of: Die Weihnachtsmänner.
Summary: When word gets around that there is no
Santa Claus, Charlie takes matters into his own hands
to prove that Santa Claus is real.
[1. Santa Claus—Fiction. 2. Christmas—Fiction.]
I. Krause, Ute, ill. II. Title.
PZ7.B78618San 1986   [E]   86-2147
ISBN 0-8037-0266-3

*The artwork for each picture consists of a black ink,
pencil, and watercolor painting, which is
camera-separated and reproduced in full color.*

The
SANTA CLAUSES

retold by ACHIM BRÖGER
pictures by UTE KRAUSE

Dial Books for Young Readers

New York

The trouble began when Mr. Smith said to Mr. Jones, "Have you heard the news? There's no such thing as Santa Claus."

"Are you sure?" asked Mr. Jones.

"Absolutely," said Mr. Smith.

Mr. Jones worked for a newspaper and since there was no other exciting news that day, he wrote a big headline that said, "THERE IS NO SANTA CLAUS!" All the other reporters saw it and copied the story in their own papers.

And that evening as Susan and Charlie were riding home on the subway, everyone was reading about it.

The news spread through the country like lightning. The adults were distressed, of course, but it was much worse for the children.

"If there's no Santa Claus, who will we send our Christmas letters to?" asked John.

"And who will bring our presents?" asked Susan.

"I just don't believe it," said Charlie. "Santa Claus *must* be real."

Actually Charlie was right. But there wasn't just *one* Santa Claus, there were several—enough to go around at Christmas among all the children in the world.

For a long time the Santas knew nothing about the news. They lived quite happily, getting ready for Christmas. Then one day their cook saw the story in a newspaper that had been used to wrap fish.

"Friends! Santa Clauses!" he shouted. "Look! It says here that there is no such thing as Santa Claus. You aren't real."

"They're crazy," said one Santa.

"How silly!" said another. "No one will believe it."

But as it got closer to Christmas, fewer and fewer letters came. The Santas were miserable. "I guess people do believe what they read in the newspaper," said one Santa, sighing.

At last they decided to call a meeting of Santa Clauses from all over the world. The invitations read,

TO SANTA CLAUSES EVERYWHERE
COME TO THE
FIRST INTERNATIONAL
SANTA CLAUS CONVENTION
URGENT!

Soon the Santas began to arrive. They came from Africa and Japan, from Europe and South America.

When they were all finally assembled, the oldest Santa stood up to speak. "Friends and fellow Santa Clauses, people are saying we're not real. All right, let's show them what it's like without us. This year we'll forget about Christmas. We'll go on strike. I, for one, have always wanted to take a winter vacation. What about you?"

"Hurrah, hurrah!" cheered all the Santas.

While the Santas were making their travel plans, Charlie was home moping around his room. Other people might forget about Santa Claus, but Charlie could not think of anything else.

Finally, just to get him out of the house, Charlie's father took him to the post office where he worked.

High up among a stack of mail Charlie suddenly saw a postcard with a sparkling gold star on it. The return address was Miami Beach.

Dear Fellow Santa,
Too bad you couldn't come with us. The weather here is perfect. Having a wonderful time. Come join us as soon as you're better.

> *Yours,*
> *The Santa Clauses*

"Wow!" thought Charlie. "You mean there's more than one?"

Right then and there Charlie made up his mind to find the Santas and bring them back in time for Christmas.

He ran home, emptied his piggy bank, and left his parents a note.

I went to get the Santa Clauses.
Love, Charlie

Then he took a bus down to the docks and spoke to the captain of a big ship. "I want to go to Miami Beach," he said. "Here's $3.32."

But it wasn't enough.

As Charlie turned a corner, he suddenly bumped into the ship's cook. *Umph!* Soon they were both rolling in potatoes.

"Everything is going wrong," the cook grumbled. "My kitchen boy has run away, my potatoes are all over the place, and lunch is supposed to be ready in an hour."

"Perfect!" said Charlie. "I'll be your new kitchen boy."

Moments later Charlie was in the ship's galley, peeling potatoes as fast as he could. A whistle sounded and the engines began to vibrate. They were on their way to Miami Beach.

After six days at sea, the ship finally arrived. "It sure is hot," thought Charlie, and he began to look for the Santa Clauses. He passed lots of hotels where there were men with white beards but he didn't see any Santas. Growing tired, he lay down under a palm tree and fell asleep. Some time later...

deep voices woke him. There were the Santa Clauses in bathing suits and sunglasses! "Why, it's Charlie," said one of the Santas. "He's on my route."

"Yes, it's me," said Charlie. "I came to get you. What's the matter? Don't you know it's almost Christmas?"

"We called a meeting," said one of the Santas.

"We're on strike," said another Santa.

"No one believes in us anyway," said a third.

Charlie put his hands on his hips and looked at them each in turn. "What about me?" he said. "I believe in you."

"Why, so you do," said all the Santas. "Okay, men, let's go!" The Santas clambered to their feet and brushed the sand from their beards. The strike was over.

Since they had got no Christmas letters, the Santas had to pick out the Christmas presents themselves. Charlie's Santa promised he could help deliver them.

On Christmas Eve the sleds were packed, the reindeer were hitched up, and they flew away among the stars. It was the best adventure Charlie had ever had.

That Christmas morning children around the world found souvenirs from Miami Beach under their Christmas trees. Each had a note attached. "You see, we *are* real. Love from the Santas."

When all the presents had been delivered, Charlie and the Santas celebrated.

"I hope they'll all believe in you now," said Charlie.

"The important thing is that you do," said the oldest Santa. "To anyone who can imagine us, we are real. It's as simple as that."

"Can I come along again next year?" asked Charlie as he said good-bye.

"Absolutely," said all the Santas. "We wouldn't have it any other way."